The Berenstain Bears
and the
Big Question

Many cubs' questions
strike grownups as odd,
but the really big one
is "Mama, what's God?"

A First Time Book®

The Berenstain Bears

Random House   New York

Copyright © 1999 by Berenstain Enterprises, Inc. All rights reserved under
International and Pan-American Copyright Conventions. Published in the
United States by Random House, Inc., New York, and simultaneously in
Canada by Random House of Canada Limited, Toronto.
www.randomhouse.com/kids   www.berenstainbears.com
Library of Congress Cataloging-in-Publication Data
Berenstain, Stan, 1923–   The Berenstain Bears and the big question /
Stan & Jan Berenstain.   p. cm. — (First time books)
SUMMARY: When Sister Bear asks her mother about God, Mama tries to explain.
ISBN 0-679-88961-2 (trade) — ISBN 0-679-98961-7 (lib. bdg.)
[1. God—Fiction.   2. Bears—Fiction.   3. Christian life—Fiction.]
I. Berenstain, Jan, 1923– . II. Title. III. Series: Berenstain, Stan, 1923– .First
time books.   PZ7.B4483Bebci   1999   99-33145
Printed in the United States of America   10 9 8 7 6 5 4 3 2 1
RANDOM HOUSE and colophon are registered trademarks of Random House, Inc.

and the
Big Question
Stan & Jan Berenstain

Early one weekend morning, Sister Bear was busy having a tea party with her dolls. She poured the tea into each of the dolls' cups. It was really apple juice. Sister didn't much care for tea. She served cookies, too.

"You're welcome, my dears," Sister said, pretending that the dolls had thanked her.

"Now," she said, folding her hands, "let's say grace."

The Bear family usually said grace before meals. Sometimes they were in such a hurry or so hungry that they forgot...especially Papa. But Mama usually reminded them.

So Sister bowed her head, closed her eyes, and said:

> *Thank you for the world so sweet.*
> *Thank you for the food we eat.*
> *Thank you for the birds that sing.*
> *Thank you, God, for everything.*

Then Sister drank her juice and ate her cookies. The dolls weren't very hungry, so Sister drank their juice and ate their cookies, too.

Later, when Sister and Mama were washing up the tea things, Sister grew thoughtful. "Mama," she said, a faraway look in her eyes, "what's God?"

Papa and Brother were just coming in from having a catch, and Papa overheard Sister's question. "That's a very Big Question, Sister," he interrupted before Mama could say anything. "It happens to be a question that people have been asking for a very long time."

Taking Sister by the hand, he led her into the living room and sat her on his knee. "Now," he said, "let me see if I can explain it to you." And then Papa began to give Sister a BIG, BORING LECTURE.

BLAH-BLAH-BLAH... BILLIONS AND BILLIONS OF STARS AND PLANETS---BLAH-BLAH---EACH IN ITS OWN APPOINTED TIME AND PLACE--BLAH-BLAH --- STRETCHED TO INFINITY---

Mama decided to step in. "That's all very interesting, Papa," she said, taking Sister off his knee. "But if you'll excuse us, Sister and I have some gardening to do."

Mama took Sister outside into the garden. It was a beautiful morning. The sun was shining, the birds were singing, and the flowers were all in bloom. "Now, Sister," Mama said as she began weeding her garden, "all you need to remember is that God made everything—the birds, the flowers, the sunshine. They're all God's work—all part of God's Great Plan."

Sister looked around at the wide, beautiful world and thought it over. "You mean," she said, "God made *everything*—everything in the whole wide world?"

"That's right, dear," said Mama.

"Did He make clouds and trees and butterflies?" asked Sister.

"Of course," answered Mama. "Everything."

But Sister didn't stop there. "Did He make worms and spiders and big yellow slugs?" she asked.

"Yes," nodded Mama, feeling a little sick as she picked a big yellow slug off her favorite geraniums. "As I said, they're all part of God's Great Plan."

"What about bellyaches?" Sister went on. "What about cold germs? What about earthquakes, floods, fires, and tornadoes?"

"Hmm!" said Mama, rubbing her chin thoughtfully. "This is an even Bigger Question than I realized!"

"Look!" said Sister, pointing to the road nearby. "There's Gramps and Gran—and they're all dressed up!"

"That's because they're wearing their Sunday-go-to-meeting clothes," said Mama.

"Good morning," said Gran. "We're going to services at the chapel in the woods. Why don't you join us?"

"Hmm," said Mama.
"Why don't we, indeed?"
Then she marched inside,
got her purse, and put on
her hat.

"Where are you going?" wondered Papa, noticing her getting ready to go out.

"*We,*" answered Mama firmly, "are all going to services at the chapel in the woods."

"Services?" said Brother as she led him down the front steps. "What's that?"

"That," explained Papa, hurrying after them, "is where we bears go when we want to think about Big Questions."

It was quiet and peaceful in the chapel—and very pretty, too. The sun shone in through windows made of bits of colored glass. Dust sparkles floated in the rays of light. An organ began to play. "Look," said Brother. "That's old Widder McGrizz playing the organ."

"Shhh!" said Mama. "The preacher's about to speak."

"Welcome, friends," said the preacher. "I'm glad to see you all here this morning. I'm especially glad to see visitors who haven't been with us before." Sister and Brother sat up. The preacher was talking about *them*.

"Now, I know you're all expecting to hear me preach," he went on. "That's why they call me the preacher." There were a few chuckles.

"But this morning," he said, "we're going to do things a little differently. Instead of me doin' the preachin', I want you to do it." The bears, all seated on long benches, looked at each other. "That's right," he said. "You do the preachin' today. Just sit there and think about the big questions of life, and when the spirit moves you, stand up and speak your piece."

It grew very still and quiet. The bench was very hard, and Sister had an itch right between her shoulder blades. But before it got too bad, someone stood up and started to speak.

It was Farmer Ben. "On this fine spring morning," he said, "I've been thinking about our beautiful Bear Country—about its woods and fields, its sparkling streams and rolling hills. I'm thankful for Bear Country. I feel thankful to God for giving us such a beautiful land in which to live." And he sat down.

The itch between Sister's shoulder blades had gone away. But now she noticed a fly crawling on the back of the bench in front of her. She wanted to swat at it. But she was afraid to make a commotion. Luckily, someone else stood up to speak.

It was Grizzly Gran. "I, too, am thankful—to see my grandcubs, Brother and Sister, here with me this morning. I feel thankful to God for two such wonderful cubs." And she sat down.

Brother and Sister felt a little embarrassed. They knew that Gramps and Gran loved them. But it had never occurred to them that their grandparents might thank God for them! Before they could feel too embarrassed, Mama was standing up to speak. "It's been a long time since I've been here," she said. "I guess we've just been too busy with everyday things. But I'm glad we came this morning. It helps me think things through." And she sat down.

The gathering lasted a little longer. Sister had a few more itches. A few more bears stood up to speak. But then it was all over, and everyone was shaking hands and talking and filing out.

The Bear family waved good-bye to Gramps and Gran and headed down the road to their tree house. Papa Bear hoisted Sister up on his shoulders to give her a ride, and Brother ran ahead, doing cartwheels to get the kinks out after sitting still for so long.

Sister Bear looked up at the clouds in the
deep blue sky and at the swallows swooping
overhead and sighed. "Mama," she said.

"Yes, dear?" asked Mama.

"What about questions?" Sister asked.

"Questions?" said Mama.

"Yes, questions," Sister repeated.
"Did God make questions?"

"Yes, Sister," Papa answered as they
came to the top of a hill and looked out
over their tree house home nestled in a
beautiful valley in Bear Country.
"*Mostly* questions."